Friends

Friends
Here...
There...
Everywhere!!!
Illustrations by
Irene Olds
Written by
Rosella Calauti
ReadersMagnet, LLC

Friends are here....

Waiting to meet, so greet those around you
with a smile and say hello!
Introduce yourself to others you may want to know.

Here is our school!

Inside we can listen and learn together!

Here is our playground!

Outside we can run, jump and play
games with our friends!
Annabel and Brie like to ride the swings instead!

Friends are there....

to help and

tell each other they care!

There are some near....

Who share their toys!

There are some faraway,

Who we must write a letter to or send an email!
Salvatore and Erika became pen pals
when, she moved away.

Friends are everywhere....

Salvatore met his best friend, Lee
when he joined the Jungle Soccer Club?
We can join clubs, that do things we think are fun too.

We have to look!

beside and between!

Friends are to the left!

Friends are off to the right!

Friends are above!

Friends are below!

Friends are down the street

at Lee's house

Climbing up a tree!

Friends are around the neighborhood!

Salvatore met Annabel, when she moved into the same apartment building.

Friends are met through the community!

Some friends remain through thick and thin!

But the best friends are those who care and those who share!

I hope to keep them my whole life through!

Making Friends is Easy

Greet those you meet,
with a smile and say hello!
Ask them how they are?
Say something nice!
Give them a chance to speak.
Listen and Share!

Making friends easy,
All you have to do is just be you.
Friends will laugh at your jokes
and help you feel good!

Reach out, there's nothing
to fear, because
Friends are here....
Friends are there....
Friends are everywhere....